If Animals Kissed Good Night

Ann Whitford Paul

Pictures by **David Walker**

Melanie Kroupa Books • Farrar, Straus and Giroux • New York

For the most kissable Hazel Jane —A.W.P.

For Ben and Ellie —D.W.

Distributed in Canada by Douglas & McIntyre Ltd.
Color separations by Chroma Graphics PTE Ltd.
Printed and bound in the United States of America by Worzalla
Designed by Irene Metaxatos
First edition, 2008
1 3 5 7 9 10 8 6 4 2

www.fsgkidsbooks.com

Library of Congress Cataloging-in-Publication Data

Paul, Ann Whitford.

If animals kissed good night / Ann Whitford Paul ; pictures by David Walker.— 1st ed.

p. cm.

Summary: Rhyming text explores what would happen if animals kissed like humans do, from a slow kiss between a sloth and her cub to a mud-happy kiss from a hippo calf to his father.

ISBN-13: 978-0-374-38051-9

ISBN-10: 0-374-38051-1

[1. Kissing—Fiction. 2. Animals—Habits and behavior—Fiction. 3. Parent and child—Fiction. 4. Stories in rhyme.] I. Walker, David, ill. II. Title.

PZ7.P278338 If 2008
[E]—dc22

2006051108

If animals kissed
like we kiss good night,

Sloth
and her cub
in late afternoon's light
would hang from a tree
and start kissing
soooo slooowwwww...

the sky would turn pink
and the sun sink down low.

Peacock and chick

would spin a fan dance
and kiss with a kickity
high-stepping prance.

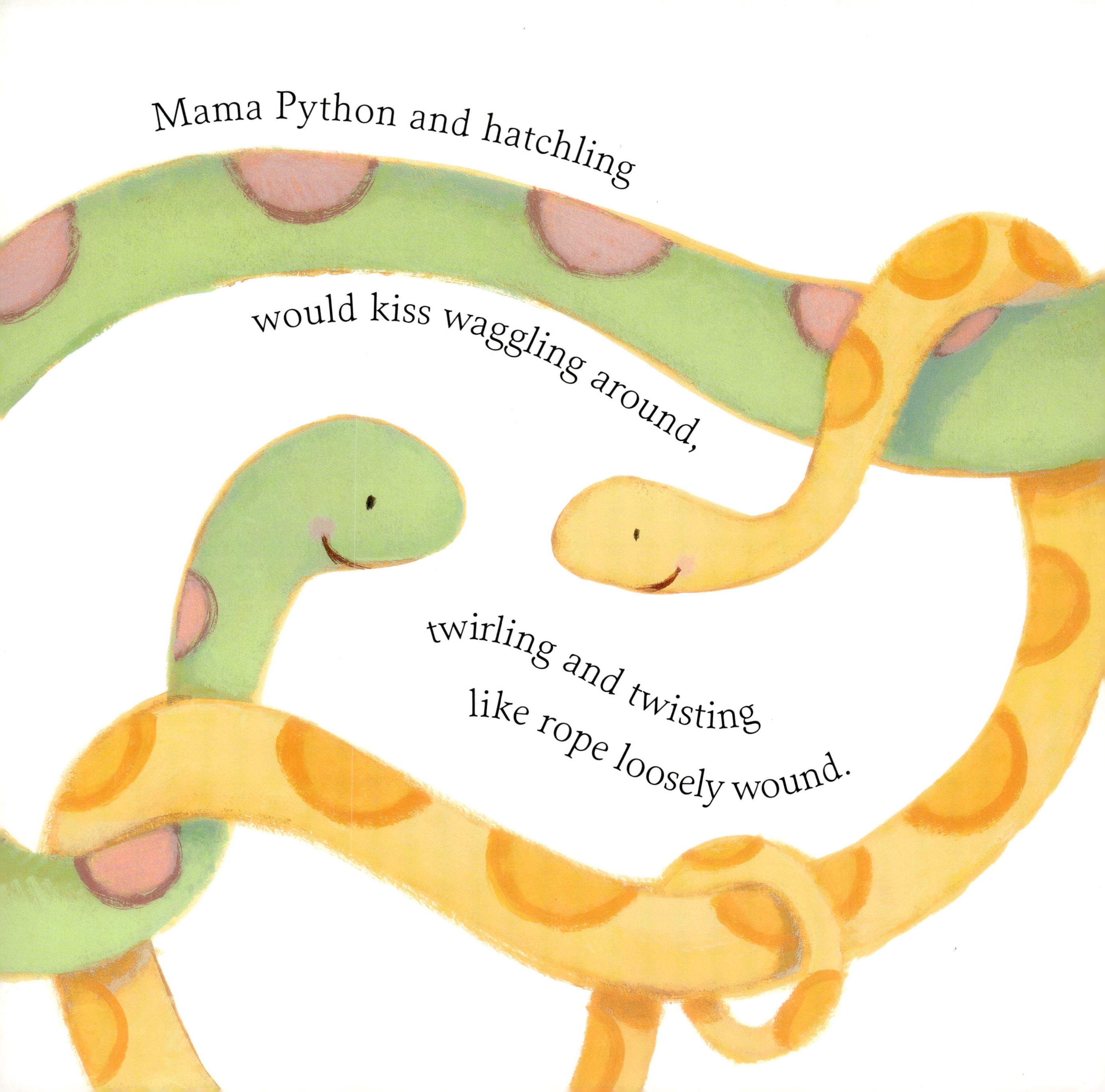

Mama Python and hatchling
would kiss waggling around,
twirling and twisting
like rope loosely wound.

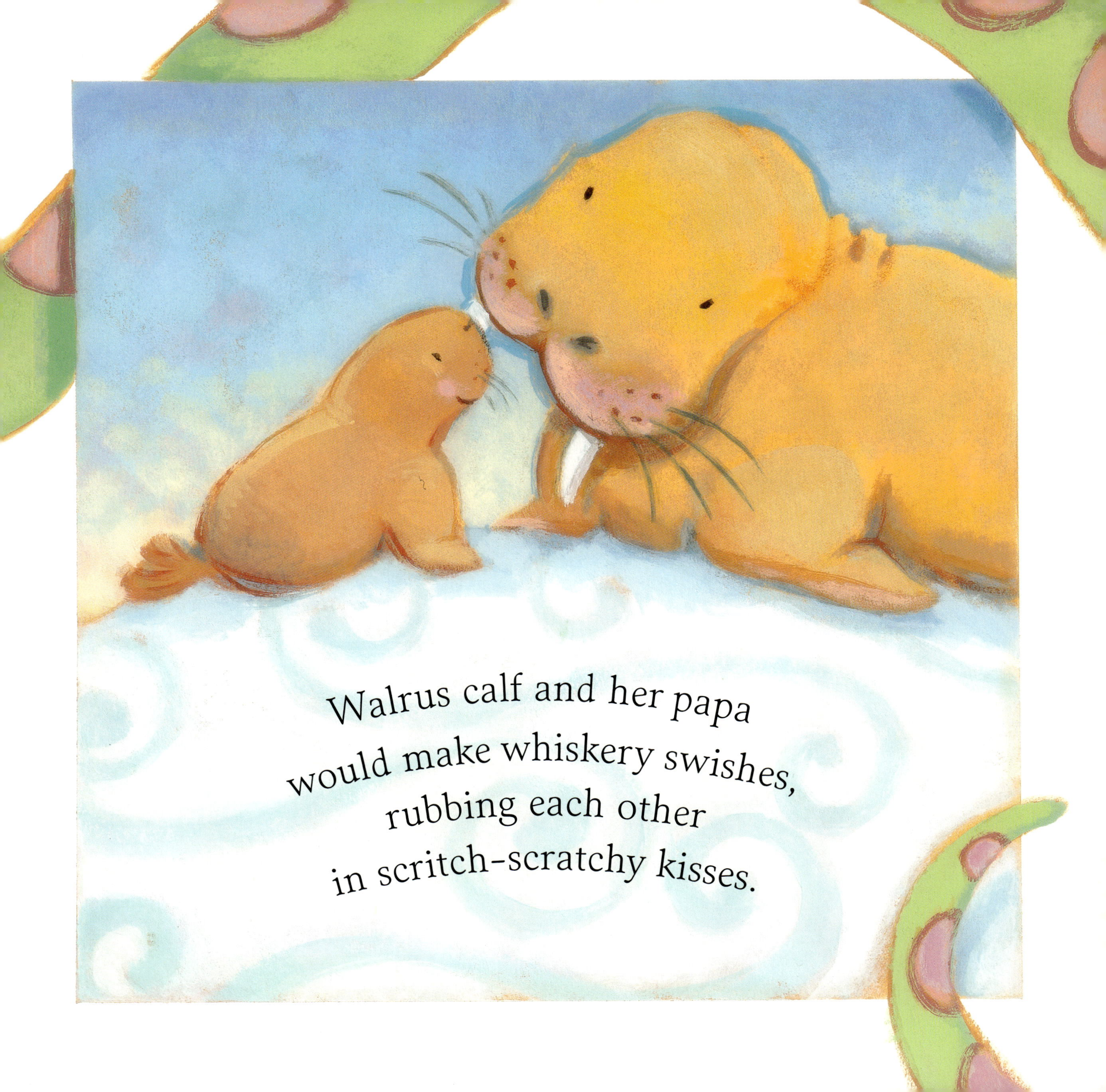

Walrus calf and her papa
would make whiskery swishes,
rubbing each other
in scritch-scratchy kisses.

Mama Elephant's trunk would kiss and then sway

and shower her calf with a wet, washing spray.

If animals kissed like we kiss good night,
the sky would turn dull, the moon a chalk white—
and Sloth and her cub?

Still . . . kissing good night.

Parrot and chick
would klick-klack their beaks,
kissing klick-a-klack,
klick-a-klack,
klick-a-klack,
kleek.

Wolf and his pup
would kiss and then
HOWL!

Bear and her cub
would kiss
and then
GROWL!

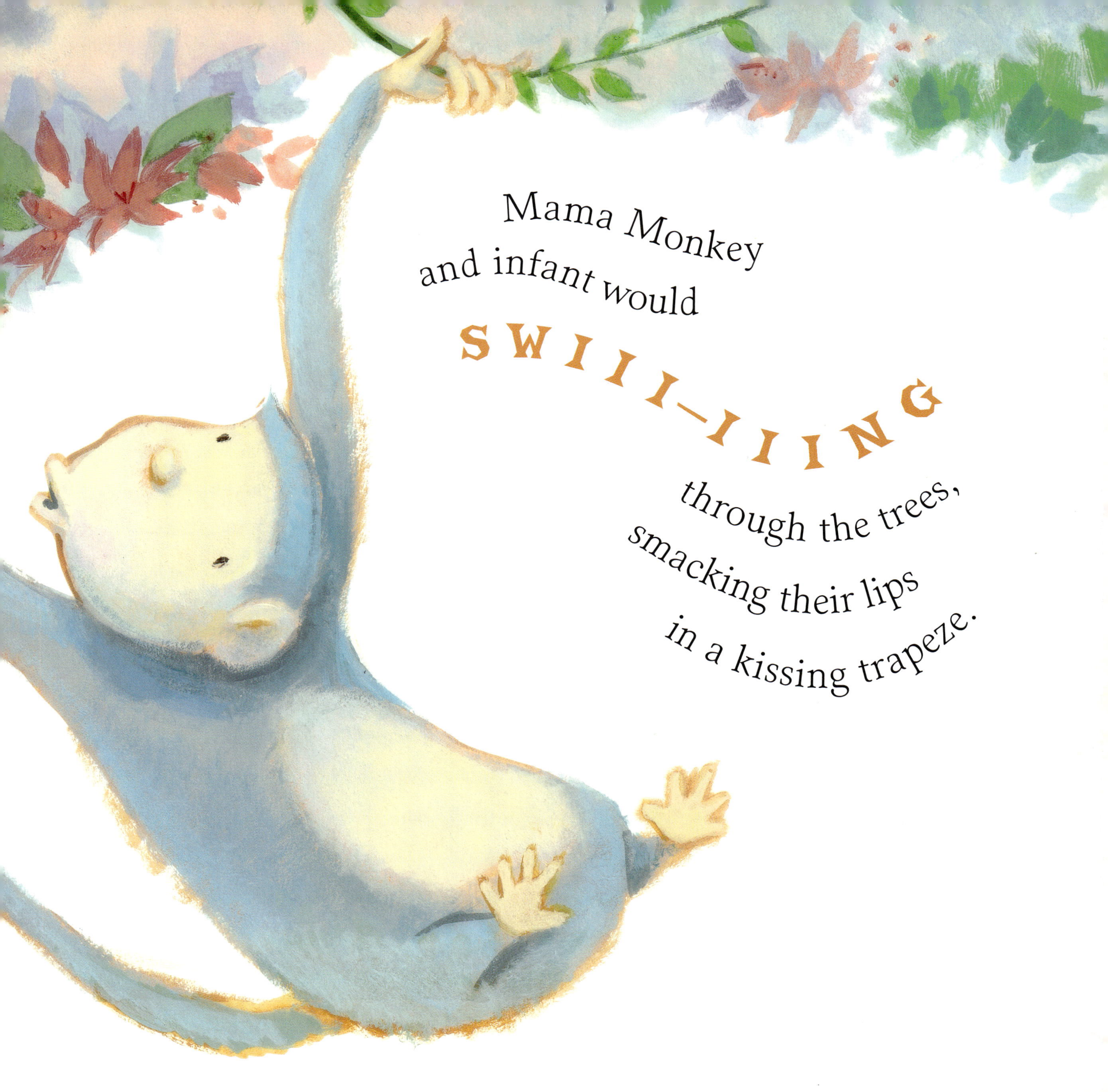

Mama Monkey
and infant would
SWIII–IIING
through the trees,
smacking their lips
in a kissing trapeze.

Seal and his calf would blow big bubbled kisses
that rise to the surface
in splashity splishes.

If animals kissed like we kiss good night,
the sky would turn dark with the moon glowing white—
and Sloth and her cub?

Still . . . kissing good night.

Mama Penguin and chick would stumble and slide

on slippery rocks in a hug-and-kiss ride.

Papa Rhino and calf
would kiss tip-a-tap-tap—
smooching their horns
in a **tip-a-tap rap.**

Giraffe
and his calf
would stretch
their necks high
and kiss
just beneath
the top
of the sky.

Kangaroo and her joey
would jumpity-jump,
kiss, kiss, kiss, kiss,
bounce bumpity-bump.

Hippo calf would kiss Papa,
then they'd settle

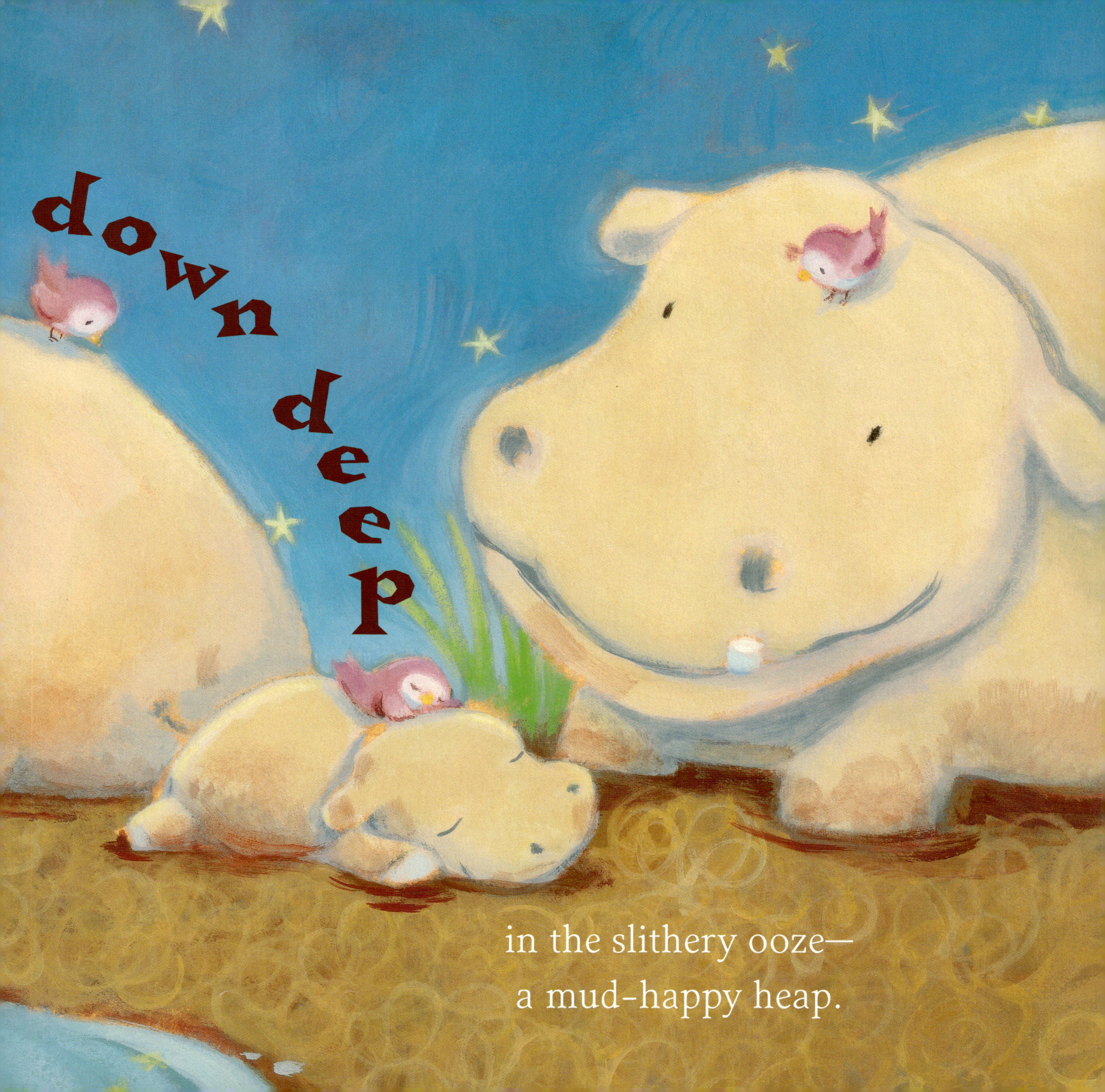
down deep
in the slithery ooze—
a mud-happy heap.

If animals kissed
like we kiss good night,

the sky would turn black,
the moon would shine bright,

all would grow quiet
with all tucked in tight—

but Sloth and her cub?

Still . . . kissing good night!